THE RARIES

JOHN TALBOT

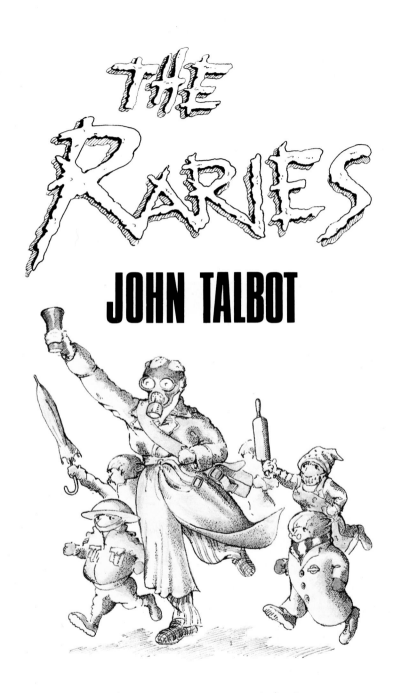

Andersen Press · London
Century Hutchinson of Australia

British Library Cataloguing in Publication Data
Talbot, John
  The raries.
  I. Title
  823'.914[J]   PZ7

  ISBN 0-86264-144-6

First published in Great Britain by Andersen Press Ltd., 62-65 Chandos Place, London WC2.
Published in Australia by Century Hutchinson Australia Pty. Ltd., 16-22 Church Street,
Hawthorn, Victoria 3122. All rights reserved. Colour separated in Switzerland by Photolitho
AG Offsetreproduktionen, Gossau, Zürich. Printed in Italy by Grafiche AZ, Verona.

Before I get any older I must tell you about something that happened when I was a boy living in London. It was during the War, and the night before my dad went off with all the other soldiers he gave me a torch and a gas-mask and said, "Sammy, be brave, and look after your mother and grandad until I get back."

When the bombs were falling at night we slept on the platforms in the Underground stations with lots of other people. It was warm and cosy down there, and we were safe.

One night, on my way back from the toilet, I heard a scuffling sound just below the edge of the platform.

Suddenly I caught a glimpse of the weirdest creature I have ever seen. "AAAAAAAAAH . . . . !"

I rushed back to where everyone was sleeping.
"Grandad, I've just seen this horrible, horrible . . . thing!"
"Was it a rat?"
"No, too big."
"Was it a spy?"
"No, too small."

"Oh, then it must have been a Rarie!"

"What's a Rarie, Grandad?"

"They're friendly little creatures that live down here in the Tube.
They're called Raries because they are so rare, and not many people
have seen one. You're very lucky, Sammy. Now go back to sleep, son."

I hadn't been asleep very long when suddenly something woke me up. All was quiet except for a small scratching sound coming from the lines. I crept over to the edge of the platform just in time to see three little creatures disappearing into the tunnel. I knew the electricity was turned off on the tracks at night, so I climbed down and made my way into the darkness.

I kept going until I could no longer see the light from the station behind me. I was just about to go back when . . . There they were! Three of them! Raries! "If we don't find him soon it will be too late," I heard one say. Who were they looking for, I wondered. Then I did a silly thing. I tripped over.

"Who's there?" one of them shouted, and before I knew what was happening they were on me. "Who are you?" "What do you want?" they yelled.

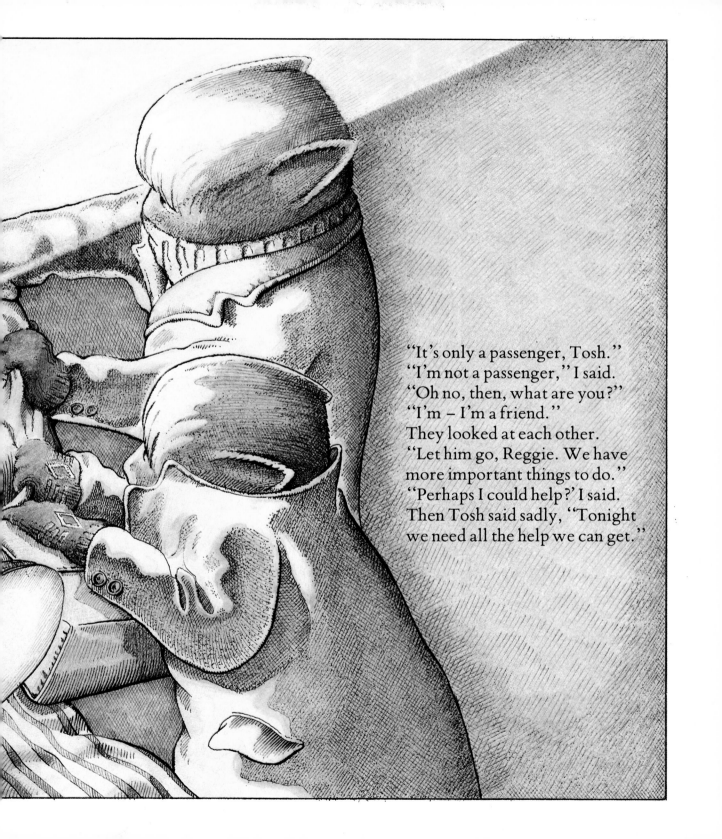

"It's only a passenger, Tosh."
"I'm not a passenger," I said.
"Oh no, then, what are you?"
"I'm – I'm a friend."
They looked at each other.
"Let him go, Reggie. We have more important things to do."
"Perhaps I could help?" I said.
Then Tosh said sadly, "Tonight we need all the help we can get."

"How do we know we can trust you?" said Reggie.

"Well . . . every time I kick my ball into our neighbour's garden, she always says, 'Trust you, Sammy', so yes, you can trust me."

"All right, come on then," he said. "But be quick, we can't hang about."

Off we went along the tracks.

"Who are we looking for?" I said at last.

"Our little nephew, Jimmy, and we think we know who has taken him."

"Who?"

"Vermin Rat! His Rat Patrol was seen going in this direction probably heading back to their dugout at Marble Arch. Now we're off to get some help from our cousins at Covent Garden."

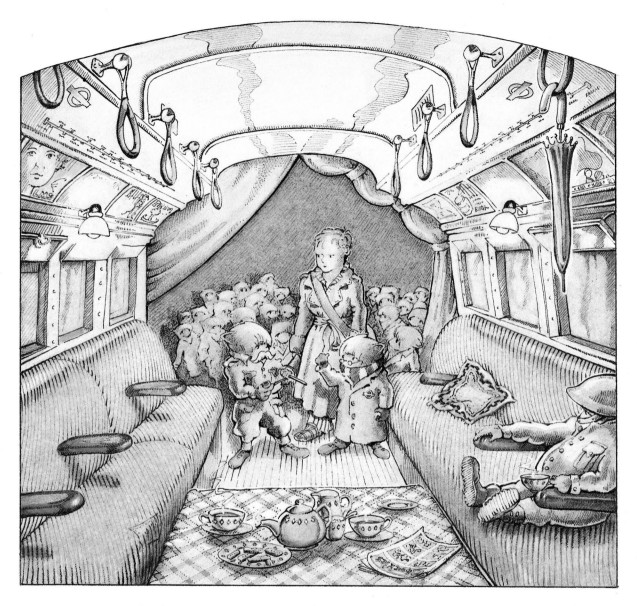

When we reached Covent Garden all the Raries stood back in surprise. Tosh took me over to their leader. "Monty," he said, "this is Sammy. He thinks he can help us find little Jimmy."

"Really?" said Monty. "What do you have in mind, old chap?"

"Well, sir," I said, "do you have a plan?"

"A plan? No, we don't have one of those. Do we, Blighty?"

"I don't think so, " said Blighty.

"I've got a plan," I said confidently, and took out my map of the Underground.

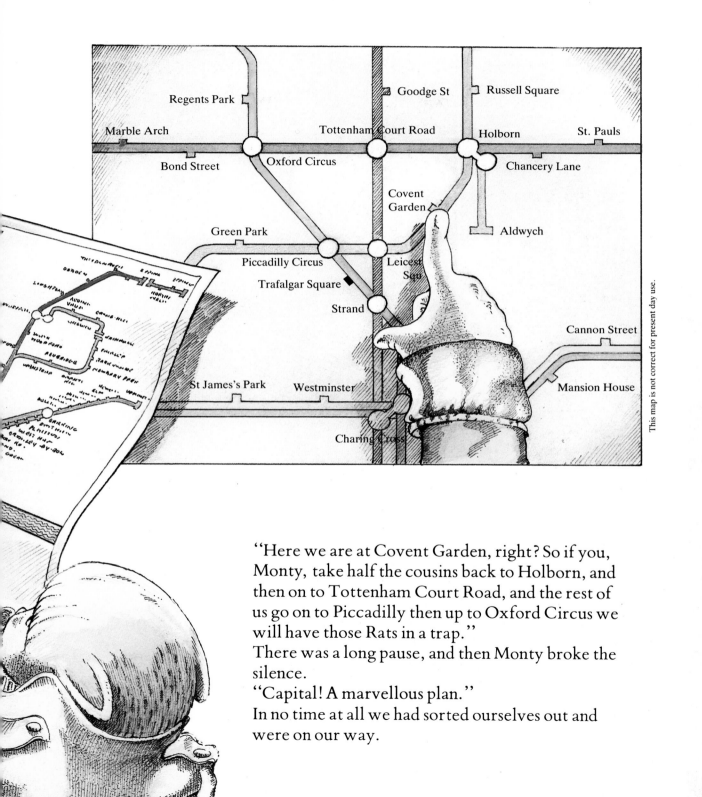

The following text appears on the map:

Regents Park

Goodge St

Russell Square

Marble Arch

Tottenham Court Road

Holborn

St. Pauls

Bond Street

Oxford Circus

Chancery Lane

Covent
Garden

Aldwych

Green Park

Piccadilly Circus

Leicester
Squ

Trafalgar Square

Strand

Cannon Street

St James's Park

Westminster

Mansion House

Charing Cross

This map is not correct for present day use.

"Here we are at Covent Garden, right? So if you, Monty, take half the cousins back to Holborn, and then on to Tottenham Court Road, and the rest of us go on to Piccadilly then up to Oxford Circus we will have those Rats in a trap."

There was a long pause, and then Monty broke the silence.

"Capital! A marvellous plan."

In no time at all we had sorted ourselves out and were on our way.

When our group reached Oxford Circus
we joined the Central Line. We hadn't gone
far when we heard the sound of marching feet.
"It's the Rat Patrol!" cried Reggie in a panic.
"Take cover!" I shouted. "And wait for the order."
When I saw Vermin Rat a cold shiver swept over me.
Then I had a BRILLIANT IDEA.

MY GAS-MASK! That'll frighten them. I put it on and stood waiting until we saw the whites of their eyes, and then I gave the order. "CHARGE!" I cried. My voice echoed all round the tunnel. "CHARGE! CHARGE! CHARGE!"

The Raries sprang from the dark into the attack. When the Rats saw us they turned and ran back the way they had come.

"They're getting away," cried Tosh.

"They won't get far!" I shouted.

We were chasing the Rats when suddenly they
turned, panic-stricken, and headed back towards us.

From the other end of the tunnel Monty and his
men were coming up fast behind them.

"Get stuck in, lads!" Monty cried, and the battle began. But the Rats were fighting dirty.

"No biting!" I shouted. "That's not fair!"

"Look!" yelled Tosh. In all the confusion Vermin Rat was running back towards the station, and getting clean away with little Jimmy as hostage.

I had almost
caught up with
them at the
platform, but my
chance came when
Vermin Rat took the
stairs. I went up on
the escalator and soon
overtook them.

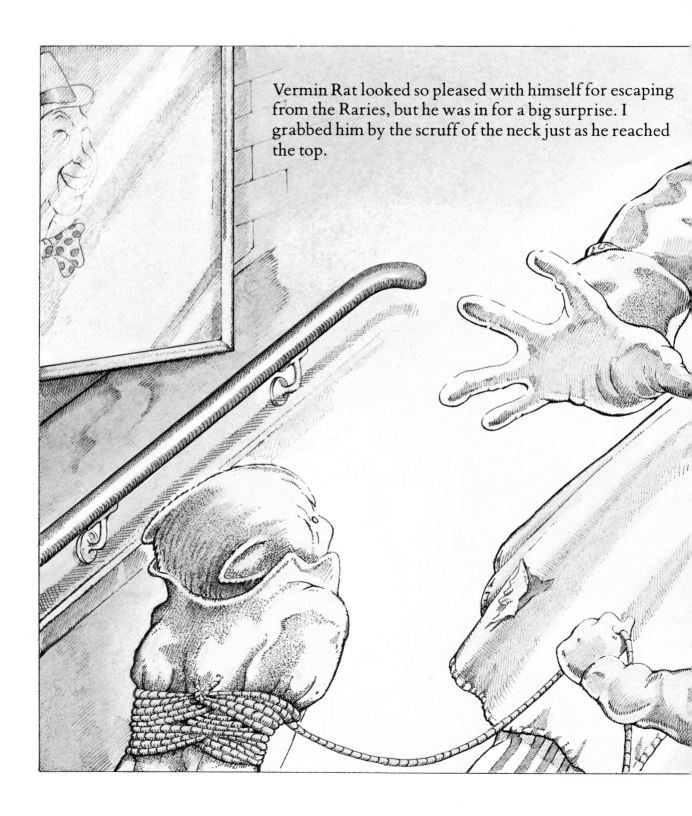

Vermin Rat looked so pleased with himself for escaping from the Raries, but he was in for a big surprise. I grabbed him by the scruff of the neck just as he reached the top.

By the time I got little Jimmy back to the others the fighting was all over and the Rats had surrendered.

"Your plan worked perfectly," said Monty, "and we want you to know how grateful we are. Don't we, chaps!"

"Hip hip," cried Blighty, and all the Raries cheered.

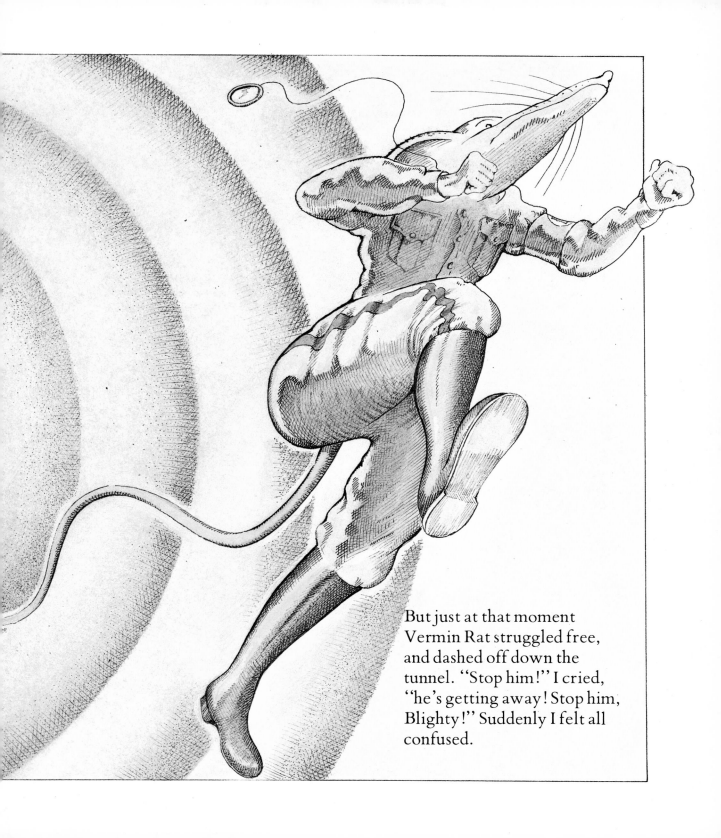

But just at that moment Vermin Rat struggled free, and dashed off down the tunnel. "Stop him!" I cried, "he's getting away! Stop him, Blighty!" Suddenly I felt all confused.

There was Grandad. And Mum was shaking me. "Wake up, son, you're only dreaming." Mum looked at Grandad. "I told you not to fill his head with silly ideas about Raries and whatnot."

"You've torn your coat, Sammy," was all Grandad said. Then he smiled, and winked at me.